The Jungle Run

Tony Mitton

Guv Parker-Rees

ORCHARD BOOKS

Here come the animals one by one,
all getting ready for The Jungle Run.

To Edith Maud Vincent,
with best jungly wishes.
– T.M

For Harper Leif,
have fun when you run.
– G.P-R

ORCHARD BOOKS
338 Euston Road, London NW1 3BH
Orchard Books Australia
Level 17/207 Kent Street, Sydney, NSW 2000

First published in 2011 by Orchard Books

ISBN 978 1 40831 174 5

Text © Tony Mitton 2011
Illustrations © Guy Parker-Rees 2011

A CIP catalogue record for this book is available from the British Library.

1 3 5 7 9 10 8 6 4 2

Printed in China

Orchard Books is a division of Hachette Children's Books,
an Hachette UK company.
www.hachette.co.uk

Cub turns up to take her place

but the others say, "You're too small to race . . ."

Parrot makes a squawk to start the fun.
And off they go on The Jungle Run.

Poor little Cub cries, "Wait for me!"
But Cub is small so the others don't see . . .

They come to the clearing
with the big vine net.
They have to go under,
so under they get.

They all
get snaggled
and tangled and caught.
The net's much trickier
than they thought!

But Cub is small so she slips straight through.

Then she takes the lead as she yells,
"Yahoo!"

They have to swing a stream
by a creeper rope.
The creeper is strong . . .
or so they hope!

The animals falter. It's scary – eek!

But Cub swings easily – what a cheek!

So, Elephant trumpets
and makes a dash.
He misses the rope!

Uh-oh . . .
Splash!

Poor old Elephant gives a groan
as the others all use him as a stepping stone.

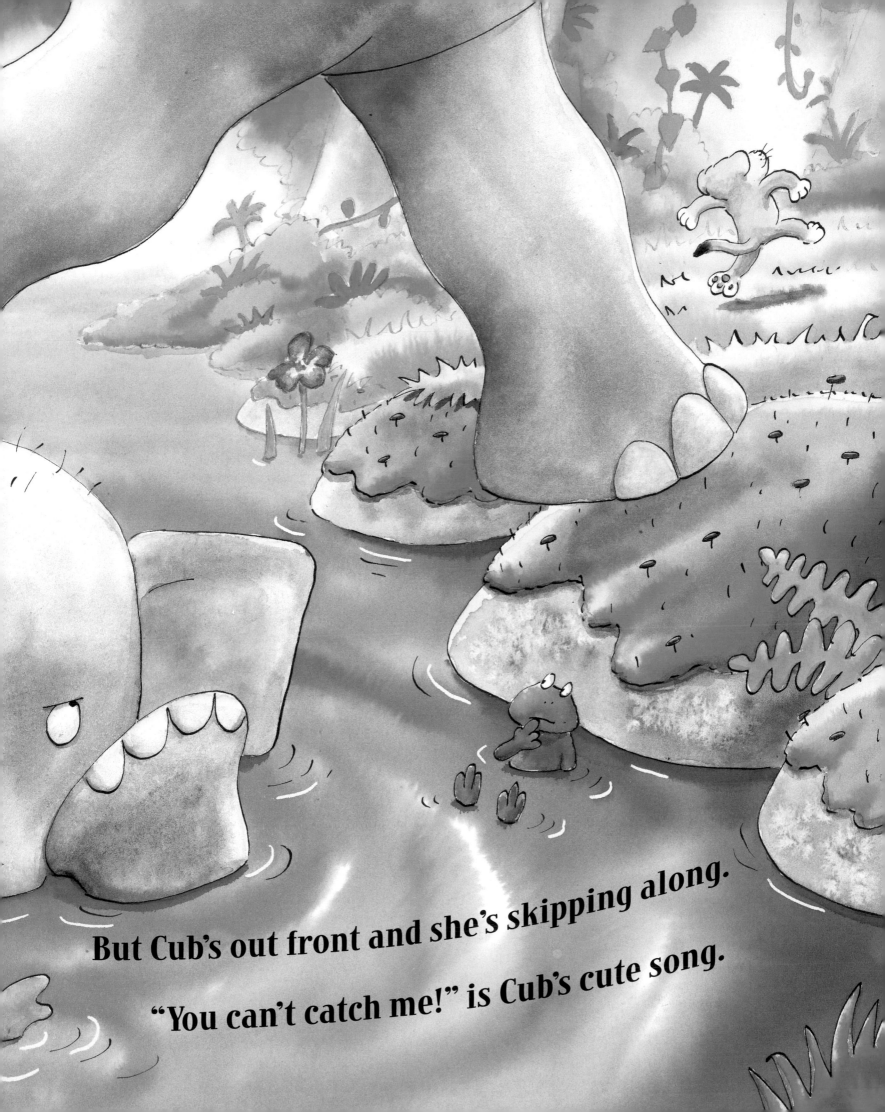

But Cub's out front and she's skipping along.

"You can't catch me!" is Cub's cute song.

At last they're coming to the end of the run.
This is the part that looks most fun.
They have to grab a mat at the top of the slide
and surf to the bottom – wow, what a ride!

They're on their mats
and they're zooming along

when, oops!

Oh dear! Something goes wrong . . .

Elephant's mat gets out of control.

He loses his balance. He's starting to roll.

They try to save him as he bounces past . . .

...but he's much too heavy and he's going too fast!

They all get caught in the speed and the swirl,

till soon they're one big animal whirl!

Oh, no! They're dropping!
They're going to crash!
Wait for it,
wait for it,
wait
for
it . . .

Splash!

They've landed safely
right in the lake.
They're at the finish.
There'll be juice and cake.

But where is Cub?

Oh, no!

Oh, dear . . .

Look! She's won and she's over here!

She grins and waves as she sings this song:

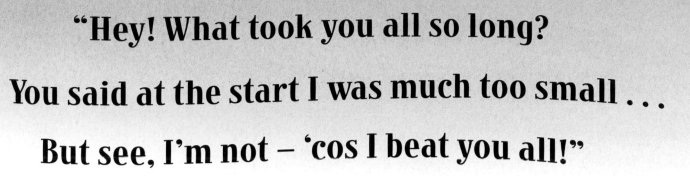

"Hey! What took you all so long?

You said at the start I was much too small . . .

But see, I'm not – 'cos I beat you all!"

The race is over and Cub has won.

and they all

But they all joined in

had fun!